The Adventures of Buster Hood

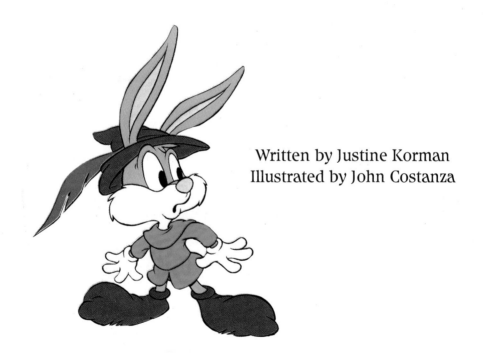

Written by Justine Korman
Illustrated by John Costanza

A GOLDEN BOOK • NEW YORK
Western Publishing Company, Inc., Racine, Wisconsin 53404

After school one day, Buster Bunny was walking home through the forest when he saw a strange crowd of ragged peasants. They were shouting, "Long live Buster Hood! Save us from the evil king!"

"Gadzooks!" said a pretty maid who looked an awful lot like Shirley the Loon. "Does not Buster Hood look fair in tights?"

"Who are these people?" wondered Buster. "Why are they dressed so funny?" Then he looked down and saw that he was wearing strange clothes, too. "Come to think of it, why am *I* dressed so funny?"

Buster asked the peasants, "Who is Buster Hood?"

"Do you not know the legend?" said fat Friar Hamton.

Buster fidgeted with his cap. "No," he said. "History is not one of my best classes."

"Indeed! You are Buster Hood of Plywood Forest," cried the fair Maid Babs. "You take from the rich and give to the poor. And we are your looney crew."

"Cool!" said Buster Hood. "But do I have to wear these silly tights?"

"Yes, and you'll need these, too," said Maid Babs, handing Buster a bow and a quiver of arrows. "Sheriff Plucky Duck is trying to capture you."

Suddenly Scout Sneezer ran into
the clearing. "Sheriff Plucky Duck
and his men are riding this way!"
he cried.

"Into the trees!" commanded
Buster Hood.

As soon as Sheriff Plucky Duck
and his men reached the thick
woods, Buster Hood's first arrow
flew straight to its mark.

"Why me?" shrieked the sheriff.

Buster Hood gave a signal, and Scout Sneezer sneezed one of his mighty sneezes to knock the evil knights off their horses.

Buster Hood emptied the gold from Sheriff Plucky Duck's saddlebags. "I hereby take back this unfair tax money," he declared. "It will be returned to the poor people of Plywood."

"You'll pay for this, Buster Hood," said the sheriff as he and his men jumped back on their horses and rode off.

Then there was a great feast in Buster Hood's camp to celebrate the victory. The fair Maid Babs played the lute and sang a ballad about Buster Hood's heroism:

"Swift as an arrow,
Brave to his marrow,
He fights for our rights
And looks great in tights."

Meanwhile, in his castle, King Montana Max roared at Sheriff Plucky Duck of Knottyham, "You lost all the tax money we took from the poor people?"

"I was ambushed by Buster Hood," Sheriff Plucky Duck explained.

"See that it doesn't happen again!" King Monty thundered. "Or I'll have your feathers for the royal duster!

"We must rid the woods of this do-goody Buster Hood," the king declared, pounding his fists on the throne.

Sheriff Plucky Duck shook his head. "That's easier said than done, sire," he said. "Buster Hood is swift as an arrow, brave to his marrow…and he even looks great in tights!"

"Never mind that!" snarled the knobby-kneed king.
"Once we lure him out of Plywood Forest, Buster Hood
will not be so tough."

Then he whispered a fiendish plan in the sheriff's
eager ear.

Back at the camp, Maid Babs was cleaning up the remains of the feast. "Alas! These noble outlaws can be such slobs," she complained. "Sometimes I wish I had been born a queen and not a maid."

Suddenly Sheriff Plucky Duck and Sir Dizzy Devil jumped from behind the trees and grabbed the fair Babs. She defended herself with her handy lute.

"Why me?" said Sheriff Plucky Duck, rubbing his dented helmet.

Fair Babs was captured and carried off to the castle of King Montana Max. There she was locked in a tall tower.

"Soon you will marry me," the evil king declared. "Then you will be Queen of all Knottyham!"

Fair Babs sighed. "I'd rather be a maid," she said.

ROYAL
ARCHERY
CONTEST
AT KING
MONTANA
MAX'S
CASTLE

Meanwhile, Sheriff Plucky Duck of Knottyham was executing Fiendish Plan Number Two. He rode through Plywood Forest putting up posters for an archery contest.

"That show-off Buster Hood will not be able to resist this contest," he muttered. "Sneaky trap, but what's a villain to do?"

The sheriff was right. Buster Hood was eager to enter the contest.

"It's a trap!" warned fat Friar Hamton.

"I know that!" said Buster. "But it's the only way for us to get into the castle and rescue the fair Maid Babs."

Buster Hood and his looney crew arrived at the archery contest wearing disguises. Buster himself wore a fake beard and a long hood.

"Spread yourselves among the crowd," Buster instructed. "We're going to make a surprise attack!"

The king's greatest archer, Sir
Calamity Coyote, shot an arrow
straight into the bull's-eye. He
proclaimed himself the winner.

"Not necessarily," said the
bearded contestant in the long
hood. The stranger let fly an arrow
that split Sir Calamity Coyote's
arrow right down the middle of the
shaft.

"Only one man could have shot that arrow—Buster Hood!" declared King Monty. "Seize him!"

The king's men quickly surrounded Buster, but at the same time the looney crew threw off their disguises. Swords clanged. Arrows flew. Then Scout Sneezer sneezed a mighty sneeze that knocked the king's evil knights to their knees.

"We give up," the dented knights declared. "King Montana Max does not pay us enough, anyway. Why fight for peanuts?"

"Let us make Buster Hood our king," suggested Elmyra the Lady Knight. "Long live the king!"

"OK," said Buster Hood. "But first you must release the fair Babs."

In no time at all, Buster Hood was wearing the royal crown—and Montana Max was washing the royal tights. The fair Babs was made queen, and Buster Hood's looney crew ate better than they ever had before.

Being king was fun for a while, but Buster Hood missed the things he was used to, like carrot shakes and pizza. Besides, he was sick of wearing tights.

"How can I get out of being king?" wondered Buster Hood as he paced up and down the throne room.

Suddenly Buster felt someone shaking him. He had
fallen asleep over his history book.

Babs Bunny was impatient. "Come on, Buster," she
said. "You have to go home and write that paper on
medieval life for school."

"I know, Fair Babs," admitted Buster Bunny with a
yawn. "But, indeed! I know exactly what to write!"